JONATHAN CAPE

UK | USA | Canada | Ireland | Australia
India | New Zealand | South Africa
Jonathan Cape is part of the Penguin Random House group of companies
whose addresses can be found at global.penguinrandomhouse.com.
www.penguin.co.uk   www.puffin.co.uk   www.ladybird.co.uk

Penguin
Random House
UK

First published 2017
001

Copyright © William Bee, 2017
The moral right of the author has been asserted

Printed in China
A CIP catalogue record for this book is available from the British Library

ISBN: 978-1-780-08050-5

All correspondence to:
Jonathan Cape, Penguin Random House Children's
80 Strand, London WC2R 0RL

williambee
Stanley's
Shop

JONATHAN CAPE • LONDON

It's going to be another busy day at Stanley's Shop.

Stanley is unloading all the fresh fruit and vegetables from the truck.

His forklift goes PEEPPEEPPEEPPEEPPEEP.

Myrtle is buying cheese from Hattie at the cheese counter.

She likes the round cheese and the square cheese and the triangular cheese. In fact Myrtle likes ANY shape cheese!

Shamus and Little Woo are doing their weekly shop. Little Woo rides in the trolley.

He is at just the right height to reach the biscuits - and the chocolate - and the bags of sweets. Little Woo LOVES shopping.

Myrtle would like some nice bread to go with all her cheese.

Gabriel gives her a loaf fresh from the oven.
Mind your fingers, Myrtle – it's still hot!

Stanley has made a beautiful display
of all the fruit and vegetables.
Well done, Stanley!

But oh dear! Charlie isn't looking
where he is going . . .

Apples, oranges, watermelons, peaches, plums, broccoli, tomatoes, onions and lovely ripe bananas . . .

. . . everywhere! Silly Charlie!

At the till Stanley scans all Shamus and Little Woo's shopping.

What a lot of biscuits and chocolate and bags of sweets!

Myrtle has bought ever such a lot of round cheese and square cheese and triangular cheese.

How can she possibly get it all home?

Luckily for Myrtle, Stanley's Shop offers home delivery . . .

Thank you, Stanley! Thank you, Hattie!

Well! What a busy day!

Time for tea!
Time for a bath!

And time for bed!
Goodnight, Stanley.

Stanley

If you liked **Stanley's Shop** then you'll
love these other books about Stanley:

Stanley the Builder   **Stanley the Farmer**

Stanley's Café   **Stanley's Garage**

Stanley the Postman